LAKE CLASSICS

Great American Short Stories III

Thomas Bailey
ALDRICH

Stories retold by Joanne Suter
Illustrated by James Balkovek

LAKE EDUCATION
Belmont, California

LAKE CLASSICS

Great American Short Stories I

Washington Irving, Nathaniel Hawthorne, Mark Twain, Bret Harte, Edgar Allan Poe, Kate Chopin, Willa Cather, Sarah Orne Jewett, Sherwood Anderson, Charles W. Chesnutt

Great American Short Stories II

Herman Melville, Stephen Crane, Ambrose Bierce, Jack London, Edith Wharton, Charlotte Perkins Gilman, Frank R. Stockton, Hamlin Garland, O. Henry, Richard Harding Davis

Great American Short Stories III

Thomas Bailey Aldrich, Irvin S. Cobb, Rebecca Harding Davis, Theodore Dreiser, Alice Dunbar-Nelson, Edna Ferber, Mary Wilkins Freeman, Henry James, Ring Lardner, Wilbur Daniel Steele

Great British and Irish Short Stories

Arthur Conan Doyle, Saki (H. H. Munro), Rudyard Kipling, Katherine Mansfield, Thomas Hardy, E. M. Forster, Robert Louis Stevenson, H. G. Wells, John Galsworthy, James Joyce

Great Short Stories from Around the World

Guy de Maupassant, Anton Chekhov, Leo Tolstoy, Selma Lagerlöf, Alphonse Daudet, Mori Ogwai, Leopoldo Alas, Rabindranath Tagore, Fyodor Dostoevsky, Honoré de Balzac

Cover and Text Designer: Diann Abbott

Library of Congress Catalog Number: 95-76745
ISBN 1-56103-063-5
Printed in the United States of America
1 9 8 7 6 5 4 3 2 1

CONTENTS

❧ Lake Classic Short Stories ❧

"The universe is made of stories, not atoms."
—Muriel Rukeyser

"The story's about you."
—Horace

Everyone loves a good story. It is hard to think of a friendlier introduction to classic literature. For one thing, short stories are *short*—quick to get into and easy to finish. Of all the literary forms, the short story is the least intimidating and the most approachable.

Great literature is an important part of our human heritage. In the belief that this heritage belongs to everyone, *Lake Classic Short Stories* are adapted for today's readers. Lengthy sentences and paragraphs are shortened. Archaic words are replaced. Modern punctuation and spellings are used. Many of the longer stories are abridged. In all the stories, painstaking care has been taken to preserve the author's unique voice.

Lake Classic Short Stories have something for everyone. The hundreds of stories in the collection cover a broad terrain of themes, story types, and styles. Literary merit was a deciding factor in story selection. But no story was included unless it was as enjoyable as it was instructive. And special priority was given to stories that shine light on the human condition.

Each book in the *Lake Classic Short Stories* is devoted to the work of a single author. Little-known stories of merit are included with famous old favorites. Taken as a whole, the collected authors and stories make up a rich and diverse sampler of the story-teller's art.

Lake Classic Short Stories guarantee a great reading experience. Readers who look for common interests, concerns, and experiences are sure to find them. Readers who bring their own gifts of perception and appreciation to the stories will be doubly rewarded.

❦ Thomas Bailey Aldrich ❧
(1836–1907)

About the Author

Thomas Bailey Aldrich was set to enter Harvard in 1852. When his father died, however, his schooling ended and he went to work.

Aldrich's father had been a wanderer, and the boy had spent his childhood in New England, New York, and New Orleans. Now it was back to New York and a job in his uncle's counting-house. But Aldrich's mind was already set on writing. He began publishing poems in magazines and meeting other authors.

When the Civil War broke out, Aldrich did not enlist in the army. He went to the front lines as a war correspondent.

At the end of the war Aldrich married and moved to Boston as editor of *Every Saturday* magazine. There the handsome newcomer with the golden-brown mustache quickly gathered a large circle of friends.

Aldrich was happy in his marriage and thrilled with his baby son. During these years he wrote his most popular story, "Marjorie Daw." He also wrote *The Story of a Bad Boy*, a novel based on his boyhood in Portsmouth, New Hampshire.

In 1881, Aldrich became editor of the *Atlantic Monthly*, a highly respected literary magazine.

Nine years later he left his job to spend more time on his own writing. By now he was well-known and wealthy. Aldrich admired the rich. But you may notice that his wealthy characters are often victims of teasing. That may be why Aldrich was once called "the Little Brother of the Rich." Who is a bigger tease than a little brother?

Can you imagine Aldrich's blue eyes twinkling as he wrote these stories?

Marjorie Daw

Delaney only meant to cheer up his sick friend. Where's the harm in that? Read on to find out.

"I CAN IMAGINE HOW YOU FEEL WITH YOUR LEG IN A CAST! IT MUST BE DARNED MISERABLE."

Marjorie Daw

I
Dr. Dillon to Edward Delaney
at The Pines near Rye, N.H.

August 8

My Dear Sir: I am happy to tell you that there is no reason for your worry. Your friend Flemming will be all right. He will have to be careful for a few weeks. A broken bone of this kind always takes a while to mend. Luckily, the bone was carefully set. I am sure there will be no lasting problems with the leg.

Flemming is doing perfectly well *physically*. I must say that his gloomy state of mind worries me. He's the last man in the world who should suffer a broken leg. You know how full of energy our friend usually is. He's never happy unless he is rushing after something— like a bull after a red flag. But it has always been easy to get along with him.

That is no longer the case. His temper has become frightful. When his sister Fanny came up from Newport to nurse him, he sent her off in tears. He has a pile of books next to his sofa. He throws one of them at Watkins whenever the loyal servant appears with his meals. Yesterday, as a little gift, I brought Flemming a small basket of lemons. You know that it was a strip of lemon peel on the sidewalk that caused our friend's fall. Well, he no sooner set eyes upon these lemons than he fell into a rage.

This is only one of his moods. At other times he sits staring at his broken leg, silent and sad. When this mood is on him—and it sometimes lasts all day—

nothing can take his mind off his problems. He will not eat. He will not read the newspapers. He has no use for books, except to use as weapons against Watkins. His state is truly a sorry one.

If Flemming continues to give in to self-pity, he will make himself sick. I'm at my wits' end to know what to do for him. Of course I have medicines to help people sleep and ease the pain. But I have no medicine that will give a man a little common sense. That is beyond my range of skills.

But maybe it is not beyond yours. You are Flemming's close friend. I'm asking you to write to him, and write to him often. Take his mind off his troubles. Cheer him up. Perhaps he has had to put some important plans aside because of his leg. If he has, you will know, and you can help him get over it. I trust that your father finds the change of scenery helpful? I am, my dear sir, with great respect, etc.

II
Edward Delaney to John Flemming
West 38th Street, New York

August 9

My Dear Jack: I had a letter from Dillon this morning. I was so happy to learn that you are going to be fine. It seems your leg is not so bad after all. Dillon will put you on your pins again in two or three weeks. You must be patient and do as he says.

I can imagine how you feel with your leg in a cast! It must be darned miserable, to be sure. And we had just promised ourselves a great month together at the seaside! But we must make the best of it. It is too bad that my father's health is poor right now. I cannot leave him. I think he is getting better. The sea air agrees with him. But he still needs my help. I cannot come to you, dear Jack. But I have hours of time on my hands. I will write you a whole post office full of letters if that will entertain you.

Heaven knows, I haven't anything much to write about. It isn't as if we are living at one of the beach houses. Then I could tell you about all the beautiful women, the sea-goddesses in their prettiest bathing suits. But we are far from all that here. The farmhouse we are renting is two miles from the hotels. We lead the quietest of lives.

I wish I were a writer. This old house would be just the place to write a summer love story. It should be a tale with the breath of the sea in it. Yet I wonder if even a love story could stir the heart of a man with pains in his leg. I wonder if the prettiest girl would be of any comfort to you in your sad shape. If I thought so, I would hurry down to the beach hotel and catch one for you!

Picture a large white house just across the road from our little cottage. It is a mansion, really, with a wide porch on three sides. It stands back from the road among some elms and oaks and weeping willows. Sometimes in the morning, and again in the afternoon, a young woman appears on the porch. She always has a book in her hand.

There is a hammock on the porch. A hammock is a very becoming picture frame for a girl of 18. Especially if she has golden hair, dark eyes, and a bright green dress. All this loveliness goes into that hammock and sways there like a perfect lily in the golden afternoon. My bedroom window looks down on that porch—and so do I.

But enough of this nonsense, Jack. Drop me a line soon, old boy. Tell me how you really are.

III
John Flemming to Edward Delaney

August 11

Your letter, dear Ned, was a blessing. Imagine what a fix I am in! I have never been sick a day since I was born. Now my left leg weighs three tons. It is blanketed in layers of cloth, like a mummy. I can't move. I haven't moved for 5,000 years.

I lie from morning until night on the sofa, staring out into the hot street. Everybody is out of town enjoying himself. The empty brownstone houses across the street look like a row of ugly coffins set up on end. Spiders have spun webs over the keyholes. All is silence and dust. Excuse me for a moment while I take aim at Watkins with a small book. Missed him! I think I could bring him down with a dictionary, if I had one. I believe that Watkins has made himself a key to the wine cellar and is having a fine time. He looks properly serious and sad when he comes into my room. But I know he grins all the way downstairs and is glad I have broken my leg.

Old Doctor Dillon worries that I have something on my mind. Nonsense. I am only tired of being off my feet. I'm not used to it. Take a man who has never had so much as a headache. Keep him in the city for weeks and turn on the hot weather. Then expect him to smile and purr and be happy! It is impossible. I can't be cheerful or calm!

Your letter is the first happy thing I've had since my fall ten days ago. It really cheered me up for half an hour. Write me, Ned, as often as you can, if you are my friend. That was very pretty, your story about the young woman who looks like a lily. I didn't know you had such thoughts in your head. I thought it was stuffed with dry legal papers rather than poetry. You really can create a picture, Edward Delaney. Perhaps, on the side, you should write love tales for magazines.

I shall be a bear until I hear from you again. Tell me more about the pretty girl across the road. What is her name? Who is she? Who's her father? Where's her mother? Who's her lover? You cannot imagine how this will keep me busy.

Being closed in has left my mind quite empty. Please write!

IV
Edward Delaney to John Flemming

August 12

My sick friend shall be entertained. But, truly, Jack, I have a hard job. There is nothing interesting here—except the little girl across the way. She is swinging in the hammock at this moment. Who is she, and what is her name? Her name is Daw. She is the only daughter of Mr. Richard W. Daw, ex-colonel and banker. Her mother is dead. They're an old, rich family, these Daws. The father and daughter live eight months of the year here. They spend the rest of their time in Baltimore and Washington. The daughter is called Marjorie—Marjorie Daw. Sounds an odd name at first, doesn't it? But after you say it over to yourself half a dozen times, you like it. Must be a nice sort of girl to be called Marjorie Daw.

I know I shall meet my neighbors before too many days more. I will surely meet Mr. Daw or Miss Daw on one of my walks. The young lady has a favorite path to the beach. I shall be there some morning and touch my hat to her. Then the princess will bend her fair head in my direction.

How oddly things happen! Ten minutes ago I was called downstairs. There I found my father and Mr. Daw greeting each other. He had come to welcome us as new neighbors. Mr. Daw is a tall, slim gentleman of about 55 years old. He has a red face and snow-white mustache. Before leaving, the gentleman offered us an invitation. He explained that Miss Daw has a few friends coming at 4 P.M. They will play croquet on the lawn and have tea on the porch. Would we honor them with our company? Having been an army colonel for many years, Mr. Daw gave us more of an order than an invitation. My father refused, saying he was not well enough. But my father's son bowed and accepted.

In the next letter, I feel I shall have something more to tell you. I shall have seen the little beauty face to face. I feel, Jack, that this Marjorie Daw is really something special! Keep up your spirits, old boy, until I write again. Let me know how your leg is doing.

V
Edward Delaney to John Flemming

August 13

The party, my dear Jack, was a real bore! A lieutenant of the navy, a man from the church at Stillwater, and a fancy gentleman from Nahant were there. The lieutenant looked as if he'd swallowed a couple of his buttons and couldn't quite get them down. The church fellow was silent. As for the gentleman from Nahant, there is little to say about him. The young women were much better. There were two Miss Kingsburys from Philadelphia, both very bright and entertaining girls. But Marjorie Daw!

The party broke up soon after tea. I stayed to talk with the colonel on the porch. It was like looking at a picture to see Miss Marjorie with the old soldier. She came and went in the summer twilight. With her white dress and pale, golden hair, she was like a lovely spirit. If she had melted into air, I should have been more sorry than surprised. It was easy to see that the old colonel loved her, and she him.

I sat with the Daws until half past ten. We watched the moon rise on the sea. It was very fine. What did we talk about? We talked about the weather—and *you*! The weather has been quite bad for several days past—and so have you. I told my friends of your accident and how it ruined our summer plans. Then I described you—or, rather, I didn't. I told them how *good* your spirits had been, how patient you were in spite of your pain! I told them of your gratitude toward Dillon and your kindness to your sister Fanny. And I told them of your man Watkins, of whom you are so fond. If only you had been there, Jack! You wouldn't have known yourself. Indeed, I see now that I would have done well defending criminals if I hadn't turned to a different branch of the law.

Miss Marjorie asked all kinds of questions about you. It struck me later, when I returned to my room, that she seemed really interested. I remembered just how eagerly she leaned forward, listening to me. Yes, I think I made her like you!

Miss Daw is a girl you would really like. I can tell you that for certain. She is a beauty who doesn't think of herself as one. She has a gentle nature. And the old colonel is a noble character, too.

I am glad the Daws are such pleasant people. We have few other neighbors here at The Pines. I'm afraid I would have found life quite boring with only my father for company.

VI
John Flemming to Edward Delaney

August 17

Say what you will about me, my friend, and I'll not complain. I don't know what I would do without your letters. They are making me well again! I haven't thrown a single book at Watkins since last Sunday. This is partly because I have grown more agreeable under your teaching, and partly because Watkins captured my weapon one night. Without a word, he carried it off to the library.

Ned, this Miss Daw must be a charming person. I should certainly like to see her. I like her already. When you spoke in your first letter of seeing a young girl swinging in a hammock, I was strangely drawn to her. I cannot explain it. What you have since written of Miss Daw has made the feeling stronger. You seem to be describing a woman I have known in some other world, or dreamed of in this. Upon my word, if you were to send me her picture, I believe I should know her. Her manner, the light hair, the dark eyes—they are all familiar to me. She asked a lot of questions, did she? Wanted to know about me? That is strange.

You would laugh at how I lie awake nights, thinking of The Pines and the house across the road. How cool it must be down there! I long for the salt smell in the air. I picture the colonel on the porch. I send you and Miss Daw off on afternoon walks along the beach. Sometimes I let you walk with her under the elms in the moonlight. You are great friends by now, I imagine. You see each other every day. Have you noticed anyone who looks like a lover hanging around her house? Does that lieutenant visit often? I wonder, Ned, why *you* don't fall in love with Miss Daw. I am about to do it myself. Speaking of pictures, couldn't you slip one of hers from her picture album? She *must* have an album, you know. You could send it to me by mail. I will return it before it could be missed by anyone. That's a good fellow!

Oh, my leg? I forgot about my leg. It's better.

VII
Edward Delaney to John Flemming

August 20

You are right. I am on very friendly terms with our neighbors. The colonel and my father sit together each afternoon. I myself pass an hour or two of the day or the evening with the daughter. I am more and more struck by Miss Daw's beauty and brains.

You ask me why I do not fall in love with her. I will be honest, Jack. I have thought of that. She is young, rich, and talented. But I'm afraid that there is something missing for me. I can't explain what it is. A woman who had it, though, could bring me to her feet. But not Miss Daw. I would like to have her for a sister and take care of her. But I do not love her. Indeed, if such feeling were there, there would still be a problem with my loving Miss Daw. Flemming, I am about to tell you something that will greatly surprise you.

The night I returned home after the party, I was thinking over the evening. I suddenly remembered how closely Miss Daw had followed my talk of your accident. I think I mentioned this to you. Well, the next morning, I went to mail my letter. And I met Miss Daw on the road to town. She joined me on my way.

Our talk turned to you. Again I noticed the interest which she had shown the night before. Since then, I have seen Miss Daw at least ten times. Every time I found that when I was not speaking of you, I was not holding her attention. Her eyes would wander away from me toward the sea. Her fingers would play with the pages of a book. She was not listening.

At these moments, I would change the subject and say something about my friend Flemming. Then her serious blue eyes would quickly come back to me.

Now isn't that the strangest thing? No, not the strangest. The feeling you had when I mentioned the girl in the hammock is certainly stranger. Is it possible that two people who have never met can be attracted to each other? I leave the answer to you. As for myself, I couldn't fall in love with a woman who listens to me only when I'm talking of my friend!

As far as I know, there is no gentleman paying special attention to my fair neighbor. The navy lieutenant sometimes drops by in the evening. But she doesn't seem interested in him.

Now about the photograph. There is a framed picture of Marjorie above the fireplace. It would be missed if I took it. I would do *almost* anything for you, Jack—but I will not go to jail for stealing.

P.S. I have enclosed a small flower from the countryside. Yes, we talked of you again last night, as usual. It is becoming a little tiring for me.

VIII
Edward Delaney to John Flemming

August 22

Your last letter has been on my mind all morning. I don't know what to think. Do you mean to say that you're really half in love with a woman you've never seen? I am confused. I understand neither you nor her. I am a down-to-earth person. I cannot understand loving someone who is no more than a shadow.

Thinking about your letter, I'm not sure it's wise for me to continue writing. But no, Jack, I will trust your good sense. Surely you know that when you do chance to meet Miss Daw, she will fall short of your dreams. Perhaps you will not care for her in the least. Please look at this in a sensible light, and I will keep no secrets from you.

Yesterday afternoon my father and I rode to Rye with the Daws. The colonel drove, and my father rode in front. Miss Daw and I sat in the back seat. I promised myself that for the first five miles I would not mention your name. First she tried to bring the subject around to you. When I wouldn't allow it, she fell silent. Then she became rather angry and began to tease me. Miss Daw can be very sweet, but she can also be disagreeable. She is like the young lady in the old nursery rhyme: "When she is good, she is very, very good, and when she is bad, she is horrid!"

On the way home, I gave in to her. I mentioned your name. By the way, I nearly forgot to say that Miss Daw had her picture taken yesterday. If it turns out well, I am going to get a copy. So now you'll get your photograph and I won't have to turn to crime.

No, Jack, the flower did not come from me. A man does not send flowers to another man. But don't get too excited. She gives flowers to everyone. She has even given a rose to me. She scatters blossoms like spring.

If my letters seem to skip around, you must understand that I never finish one

at a sitting. I write from time to time
when I am in the mood.

I am not in the mood now.

IX
Edward Delaney to John Flemming

August 23

I have just returned from the strangest
meeting with Marjorie. She all but said
right out that she is interested in you. It
was not so much her words that said it,
but her manner. But by now, nothing
surprises me.

It is past midnight, and I am too sleepy
to write more.

Thursday Morning

My father has decided we should spend
a few days away. In the meantime you
will not hear from me.

X

Edward Delaney to John Flemming

August 28

We returned to The Pines only this morning. I found on my desk three letters from you! Dear Flemming, I believe that as your leg grows stronger, your head grows weaker! But as you ask my advice, I will give it. I think that you would be very unwise to write a note to Miss Daw, thanking her for the flower. She knows you only through me. To her, you are a figure in a dream.

You say, with the help of a cane, you are able to walk about your room. You say you mean to come to The Pines the minute Doctor Dillon thinks you can make the trip. Again, *I ask you not to*. The longer you stay away, the more interested Marjorie becomes. Your hurry will ruin everything. Wait until you are completely well. Do not come without giving me warning.

Miss Daw was glad to see us back

again. It is too bad that the photographer ruined the picture. She will have to give him another sitting. I believe that something is bothering Marjorie. She does not seem herself.

I must end now, to accompany my father on one of his walks.

XI
Edward Delaney to John Flemming

August 29

I write to tell you what has happened since my letter of last night. One thing is clear—you must not dream of coming to The Pines. Marjorie has told her father everything! Now the colonel is angry. It seems he was hoping to match his daughter with the navy lieutenant. I don't know what Marjorie told him, but he is angry at *me*. I don't see why. I don't see that *anybody* has done anything wrong.

Nevertheless, it is likely that the friendship between the two houses will be broken off. I will let you know what happens. We shall stay here until the second week in September. Stay where you are. Do not dream of joining me. Colonel Daw is standing on the porch looking rather wicked. I have not seen Marjorie today.

XII
Edward Delaney to
Thomas Dillon, M.D.
Madison Square, New York

August 30

My Dear Doctor: If you have any power over Flemming, I beg you to keep him from coming to this place. I will explain everything to you before long. If you keep him in New York, you will be doing both him and me a real service. Please do not mention my name in this matter. You know me well enough to know I have good reasons. We shall return to town on the 15th of next month. I will explain everything then. I am glad to say my father is nearly completely well.

XIII
Edward Delaney to John Flemming

August 31

Your letter, stating your mad plan to come here, has just reached me. Please stop and think a moment. The step would hurt your interests and hers. You would anger her father. Though he loves Marjorie dearly, he does not like to be crossed. You do not want him to treat her badly. That is what would happen if you came to The Pines.

We must be careful, Jack. A mistake now could cost us the game. If you consider the prize worth winning, be patient. Trust me. Wait and see what happens. Moreover, Dillon writes that you are in no shape to make so long a trip. He thinks the sea air would be bad for you. Listen to me, dear Jack. Listen to Dillon.

XIV
Telegrams

September 1

1. To Edward Delaney

Letter received. Dillon be hanged. I think I should be there.

J. F.

2. To John Flemming

Stay where you are. You would only make matters worse. Do not move until you hear from me.

E. D.

3. To Edward Delaney

My being at The Pines could be kept secret. I must see her.

J. F.

4. To John Flemming

Do not think of it. It would be useless. Mr. Daw has locked M. in her room. You would not be able to see her.

E. D.

5. To Edward Delaney

Locked her in her room! That settles the question. I shall leave on the next train.

J. F.

XV
The Arrival

On the second of September a young man stepped from the station platform. He leaned on the shoulder of a servant whom he called Watkins. Then he got into a carriage and asked to be driven to The Pines.

They arrived at the gate of a simple farmhouse. With a good deal of trouble, the young man climbed from the carriage. He looked quickly across the road. He seemed very interested in something about the landscape. He leaned again on his servant's shoulder, and together they walked to the door of the farmhouse. There he asked for Mr. Edward Delaney. The old man who answered his knock reported that Mr. Edward Delaney had gone to Boston the day before. Only Edward's father, Mr. Jonas Delaney, was within. Edward had left a letter, however, for a Mr. Flemming.

XVI
Edward Delaney to John Flemming

September 1

I am horror-stricken at what I have done! When I began these letters, I meant only to entertain you. Dillon told me to cheer you up. I tried. I thought you were just playing along. I had no idea, until much later, that you were taking matters so seriously.

What can I say? I am a dog. I tried to create a little romance, something soothing and peaceful, to interest you. But I have done it only too well! My father doesn't know a thing about this. So please don't upset the old gentleman if you can help it. I've run away from your anger!

Oh, dear Jack, I'm sorry. There isn't any mansion on the other side of the road. There isn't any porch. There isn't any hammock. And there isn't any Marjorie Daw!

A Struggle for Life

Philip prayed that someone would find him. But who would look for a living man in a cemetery?

PHILIP HAD NOT HEARD THE SAD NEWS BEFORE HE
ARRIVED. JULIE DORINE WAS DEAD!

A Struggle for Life

One morning last April I was passing through Boston Common on the way to my office. I saw a certain gentleman there. Usually I'm busy with my own thoughts and pay no mind to others. But something about this man's face caught my eye.

It was a very unusual face. The man's eyes were faded. His long hair was marked with gray. His hair and eyes, if I may say so, were 70 years old. But the rest of him was not even 30. His body and his walk were young while his head and face seemed to be old. This strange combination drew more than one curious look. He was an American, that was clear. And he looked like a man who had seen something of the world, this fellow who was strangely old and young.

Before reaching the Park Street gate, I'd returned to my own thoughts. Yet throughout the day, this old-young man glided like a ghost through my mind.

The next morning I saw him again. This time he was resting against green rails. He was watching two small boats which had drifted out to sea. The helpless owners were running up and down the shore, worrying how to get them back. From the look on his face, I wondered if these two boats were somehow making him think of his own losses.

"I would like to know that man's story," I said, half aloud.

"Would you?" replied a voice at my side. I turned. There stood Mr. Hall, a neighbor of mine. He laughed loudly at finding me talking to myself. "Well," he added, "I can tell you this man's story. If you can come up with a stranger tale, I shall be glad to hear all about it."

"You know him, then?" I asked.

"Yes and no," Hall said. "I happened to be in Paris when he was buried."

"Buried!" I said.

"Well, not exactly buried, I suppose. But something quite like it. If you have a half-hour, I'll tell you all I know," Hall went on. "The affair made some noise in Paris a couple of years ago. The gentleman himself, standing over there, will serve as a picture for this tale."

The following pages tell the strange story that Mr. Hall told me. While he was telling it, a gentle wind came up. The tiny boats drifted about the ocean. The poor owners flew from point to point, hoping the breeze would blow their boats to either shore. Now and then early robins sang from the elms. And the old-young man leaned on the rail in the sunshine. He could not dream that two gossips just 20 yards away were talking about him.

* * *

Three people were sitting in a room whose large window overlooked a Paris street. M. Dorine was at one end of the room. He kept his eyes on his newspaper. He was careful not to glance toward the sofa on his right. Seated there was Mademoiselle Julie Dorine and a young American gentleman. His handsome face clearly showed his feelings for the lady.

There was not a happier man in Paris that afternoon than Philip Wentworth. Life had become so wonderful to him that he hated to look beyond today. What could tomorrow possibly add to his full heart? What might it not take away? The deepest joy often has this note of sadness in it. It is a feeling without a name, this fear that such happiness must surely end.

Wentworth was aware of this shadow that night. He stood and held Julie's hand to his lips for a moment before he left. His face was serious. Anyone watching would not have guessed that he was the happiest man in Paris.

M. Dorine laid down his paper and

came forward. "If the house is as fine as M. Martin says it is, you should buy it at once," he said. "Remember, the last train back here leaves at five. Be sure not to miss it. We have fine seats for a play tomorrow night. Ah, but tomorrow night!" he laughingly added. "It seems such an age from now when you are deeply in love."

The next morning the train took Philip to a lovely spot within 30 miles of Paris. An hour's walk through green lanes brought him to M. Martin's house. In a kind of a dream, the young man wandered the rooms and looked over the stable and the lawns. After dining with M. Martin, Philip bought the house. He returned to the station just in time to catch the train.

Soon the lights of Paris came into sight. It seemed to Philip that years had passed since he left Paris. On reaching the city, he drove to his hotel. There he found several letters lying on the table. He did not bother to look at them.

Philip was in such a hurry to see

Mademoiselle Dorine that his coach seemed to creep along the streets. At last it drew up before M. Dorine's house. The door opened as Philip's foot touched the first step. The servant quickly took his coat and hat. But he seemed oddly quiet, Philip thought.

"M. Dorine cannot see you at present," the servant said slowly. "He wishes you to be shown up to the salon."

"Is Mademoiselle . . ."

"Yes, Monsieur," the servant said.

"Alone?"

"Alone, Monsieur," repeated the man.

Philip could hardly hold back a cry of happiness. It was the first time he had been allowed to meet with Julie alone. Always before M. Dorine or some other member of the household had been present. But this is the way it is when one is courting a French girl from a fine family.

Philip did not wait a second longer. He flew up the steps, two at a time. He hurried through the softly lighted hall. He could smell her favorite flowers as he opened the door of the salon.

The room was darkened. In the center stood a slim black casket. A lighted candle and some white flowers were on a table nearby. Julie Dorine was dead.

M. Dorine heard the terrible cry ringing throughout the house. He hurried from the library. In a moment he found Philip standing like a ghost in the middle of the room.

It was not until later that Wentworth learned what had happened. On the night before, Mademoiselle Dorine had gone to her room. Seeming perfectly well, she asked her maid to wake her early the next day. When the girl came to her room in the morning, Mademoiselle Dorine, sitting in a chair, appeared to be asleep. The candle had burnt down and a book lay open at her feet. The girl saw that the bed had not been slept in. Then she noticed that her mistress was still wearing her evening dress. She rushed to Mademoiselle Dorine's side and found that she was not asleep. She was dead.

Two messages were sent at once to

Philip. One went to the train station, the other to his hotel. The first missed him. The second, he had not opened. When he arrived at the house, the servant believed that Wentworth had already learned the sad news. So he showed him directly to the salon.

Crowds came to the final ceremonies for the lovely Mademoiselle Dorine. Her body was to be laid in M. Dorine's tomb, in the cemetery of Montmartre.

I must describe the tomb. First there was an iron grating. Through this you looked into a small hall. At the end of the hall a heavy oak door opened upon a short flight of stone steps. These went down into the tomb. The tomb itself was 15 or 20 feet square. Air rushed in from somewhere in the ceiling, but there were no lights. Within the tomb were two caskets. The first one held the remains of Madame Dorine, who had died long ago. The other one was new. On its side were the letters J.D.

A wax candle burned at the foot of the casket. By its flickering light, the lid was gently closed. Then the sad party left, and the oak door closed on its old hinges.

M. Dorine threw himself into his carriage. He was filled with grief. He did not notice that he was alone in the back seat. The sound of wheels turning rattled on the road. Then all was silent again in the cemetery of Montmartre.

But it is not with that carriage that our interest lies. And it is not with the dead in her mysterious dream. Our interest lies with Philip Wentworth.

The rattle of wheels had died out when Philip opened his eyes. He stared into blackness. Where was he? In a second the truth flashed upon him. He had been left inside the tomb! While kneeling on the farther side of the casket, he must have fainted. In the sad ceremony, his absence had not been noticed.

His first feeling was one of fear. But this passed as quickly as it came. He no longer loved life so very much, after all. Just that morning he had wished he could die along with Julie. Then he shook his head and thought of his dear mother.

Wasn't he a coward to give up the life his mother had loved? Wasn't it his duty to fight to live if he could?

He had a strong spirit. The fear of the grave found no room in his heart. He was simply shut in a room and had to get out. In fact, it gave him comfort to know that Julie's body was with him. Perhaps her spirit would protect him.

Philip happened to have a box of wax matches in his pocket. After several tries, he lit one against the damp wall. By its dim light, he saw that a candle had been left in the tomb. Now he lit the candle and held it up to the oak door. The door was solid. He could never get it open.

He put the candle on the floor and watched the blue flame flicker. "At least the place has air," he thought. Suddenly Philip jumped forward and blew out the light. He needed that candle!

Once he had read about a shipwreck. By eating a few candles, the people had lived for days. And here he had been burning away his very life!

By the light of one of the matches, he

looked at his watch. It had stopped at eleven o'clock. But was it eleven o'clock that day, or the night before? He knew the funeral had left the church at ten o'clock. How many hours had passed since then? How long had he been in a faint? Alas! It was no longer possible for him to measure time. Hours crawl like snails to the miserable!

Philip picked up the candle and sat down on the stone steps. Escape did not seem likely. Of course, he would be missed. His friends would search for him. But who would think of looking for a living man in the old cemetery of Montmartre? They might drag the River Seine and look at the bodies at the police station. But he would be here—in M. Dorine's family tomb!

Yet, it was *here* that he was last seen. A smart detective might remember that. Or perhaps M. Dorine would send fresh flowers to replace those that now filled the tomb with their sweet smell. But if one of those things did not happen soon, it might as well *never* happen. How long could he stay alive with no food or water?

Quietly, he cut the half-burned candle into four parts. "Tonight," he thought, "I will eat the first of these small pieces. Tomorrow, I'll eat the second. Tomorrow evening, the third. The next day, the fourth. And then I'll wait."

He had eaten no breakfast. Now he was terribly hungry. He put off eating for as long as he could. He figured it must have been near midnight when he ate the first of his four meals. The bit of white candle wax had no taste, but it served its purpose.

He was no longer hungry. But he found a new problem. The damp walls and the wind that crept in had chilled him to the bone. He kept walking in circles, but a sleepiness was coming over him. It took all his will to fight it off. To sleep, he felt, was to die. Philip Wentworth had made up his mind to live.

Strange thoughts went through his head. He saw faces from long ago, heard voices he hadn't heard in years. His life passed before him in pictures. The sleepiness had finally left him, but he was hungry again.

It must be near morning now, he thought. The sun is just lighting the rooftops of Paris. *Paris!* The very word seems like a dream. Did he ever walk in its gay streets in the golden air?

Philip knew that the dark gloom, the silence, and the cold were getting the best of him. He sank down on the steps and thought of nothing. His hand fell on one of the pieces of the candle. He ate it. This made him feel a bit better. "How strange," he thought. "Not a drop of water has passed my lips for two days. And still I am not thirsty! Thank Heaven that sleepiness has gone. I think I was never more wide awake than I am right this minute."

The minutes passed like hours. For a while Philip walked quickly up and down the tomb. Later he rested against the door. More than once he felt like falling upon Julie's coffin and giving up his fight for life.

Only one piece of candle was left. He

had eaten the third piece to keep the hunger from returning. Soon even this poor food would be gone. The half-inch of candle that he held in his hand was dear to him. It seemed to be his last defense against death.

At last, with a sinking heart, he raised it to his lips. Then he stopped. He threw the piece across the tomb. Then suddenly the oak door was flung open! With dazzled eyes, he saw M. Dorine outlined against the blue sky.

M. Dorine led Philip out, half-blinded, into the daylight. He noticed that Philip's hair, once as black as a crow's wing, was now streaked with gray. His eyes, too, had faded. The darkness had dulled their light.

"And how long was he really locked in the tomb?" I asked, as Mr. Hall ended the story.

"*Just one hour and twenty minutes!*" replied Mr. Hall, smiling.

* * *

Now the little boats, with their sails blown out like white roses, came floating bravely to port. Philip Wentworth watched them, wearily, in the April sunshine.

I could not forget Mr. Hall's story. Here was a man who had gone through the strangest experience. Eighty minutes had seemed like two days to him! I think if he really had been locked up for two days in the tomb, the story would have been less unusual.

Of course, after this, I looked at Mr. Wentworth with deepened interest. Every day, as I met him on the Common, something in his loneliness touched me. I decided to speak to him one May morning when we met on the path. He had stopped to let me pass.

"Mr. Wentworth," I began, "I . . ."

He broke in. "My name, sir," he said in a formal manner, "is Jones."

"Jo-Jo-Jones!" I gasped.

"Not Jo Jones," he returned coldly. "Frederick Jones."

Mr. Jones, or whatever his name is, will never know why another man called him "Mr. Wentworth." He will never know why the man quickly rushed down the path and disappeared into the crowd. Unless, that is, he reads these pages.

The fact is that I had been fooled by Mr. Hall. Why hadn't I known that? I knew that Mr. Hall sometimes writes stories for magazines. But at the time I had no idea that he was actually trying out one of his tales on me!

As I later learned, my hero is no hero at all. He is an ordinary young man. He had something to do with building that pretty rock bridge in the Public Garden.

Sometimes I think of how coolly and quickly Mr. Hall built his story—and how easily I believed it. I almost want to laugh. Although I feel more than a little angry at having been such an easy victim of his Black Art.

❧❧❧

Mademoiselle Olympe Zabriski

A young man from high society could never fall in love with a common circus performer. Or *could* he?

MADEMOISELLE ZABRISKI WAS AN ATHLETE OF GREAT
GRACE AND BEAUTY.

Mademoiselle Olympe Zabriski

Chapter I

People often joke about the way women gossip. As if that sin—if it *is* a sin— belonged only to females! By no means could *males* do such a thing! However, so far as I can see, men are as much given to small talk as women.

If it came to a matter of pure gossip, I would back Our Club against any women's club there is. Sometimes four or five young fellows sit about our drawing room, talking and laughing. When that happens, you may be sure

they are bringing their heads together
for some gossip. They are discussing
Tom's engagement or Dick's spending
habits. Or perhaps they're talking about
Harry's hopeless love for *both* the young
Miss Fleurdelys. In short, it is here that
everything is covered. Everything that
happens in our group, I mean. And much
is also said that never happens—and a
great deal that could not possibly
happen. It was at Our Club that I
learned about the Van Twiller affair.

It was great entertainment, the Van
Twiller affair. But it was also a rather
unhappy thing, I think, for Van Twiller.
To understand the case fully, you must
understand Ralph Van Twiller. He is one
of the proudest and most sensitive men
alive. He is a descendant of Wouter Van
Twiller, the famous old Dutch governor
of New York—New Amsterdam, as it was
then. His mother is Mrs. Vanrensselaer
Vanzandt Van Twiller. As you sail up the
Hudson, her huge mansion will be
pointed out to you on the right bank.

Ralph is about 25 years old. Birth

made him a gentleman. The rising value of real estate made him a millionaire. It must have been a kind fairy that stepped in and also made him a good fellow. Fortune must have been in her best mood when she heaped her gifts on Van Twiller. He was, and will be again, the pride of Our Club. He will, that is, when this dark cloud blows over.

It was about a year ago that a whisper, a simple breath, came floating through the billiard room. Van Twiller was in some kind of trouble. For some reason, it became the fashion for everybody to speak of Van Twiller as "a man under a cloud." But what the cloud was and how he got under it were facts that no one seemed to know. It surely was not a problem of money. Was he in love? That didn't seem likely. If he had been in love, all the best families would have known about it right away.

"He has the signs of being in love," said Delaney, laughing. "I remember once when Jack Flemming . . . "

"Ned!" cried Flemming. "Be quiet

about that silly business."

This was one night when Van Twiller had wandered into the club. He glanced at the books in the reading room and wandered out again without speaking ten words. Anyone could see that a great change had come over him. Once, if you went to two or three places in an evening, you were sure to meet him everywhere. Now you rarely met him anywhere.

By and by came whisper number two. This time the whisper said that Van Twiller was in love. But with whom? The list of possible Mrs. Van Twillers was carefully gone over. Then that small voice of rumor came again. But this time it had a sharpness to it. It said that Van Twiller was in love *with an actress*! Van Twiller, the flower of his fine old family, in love with an actress! That was too silly to be believed—and so everybody believed it!

Six or seven members of the club suddenly discovered a new interest in drama. In groups of two or three they stormed all the theaters in town. But no clue could be found to Van Twiller's

mysterious love. After several weeks of
this, Delaney and I thought we caught
sight of Van Twiller one night. We were
almost sure we saw him in the private
box of an uptown theater. Some daredevil
trapeze show was going on that we did
not care to sit through. But later, we
decided that it was only somebody who
looked like him.

There was clearly a real mystery
surrounding Van Twiller's romance. That
left us free to come up with the wildest
ideas. Everyone agreed, however, that
Van Twiller was on the point of making
an awful match.

Up to this time he had visited the club
often. Suddenly he no longer appeared.
He was not to be seen on Fifth Avenue
or in Central Park. His rooms—and
mighty comfortable rooms they were—
on 34th Street were empty. He had
dropped out of the world.

The following talk took place one night
in the smoking room:

"Where's Van Twiller?"

"Who's seen Van Twiller?"

"What's become of Van Twiller?"

"It strikes me that you fellows are in a great fever about Van Twiller," Frank Livingstone said.

"So we are."

"Well, he's simply gone out of town."

"Where?"

"Up to visit the old homestead on the Hudson."

"It's an odd time of year for a fellow to visit the country."

"He has gone to visit his mother," said Livingstone.

"In February?"

"I didn't know, Delaney, that there was any law stopping a man from visiting his mother in February."

Livingstone was in tight with Van Twiller. If any man shared his secrets, it was Livingstone. He knew about the gossip that had been spreading around the club. But he explained nothing. Perhaps he had promised to keep silent. Or maybe he didn't think it worth his time to put our curiosity at rest. Then, suddenly, it was reported that Van

Twiller was going to Europe. And so he did. A dozen of us went down to the docks to see him off. It was refreshing to know something certain about Van Twiller at last.

Chapter II

Shortly after Van Twiller sailed for Europe, the whole thing came out. Maybe Livingstone found the secret too heavy to carry after all. Maybe it came directly from the mouth of Mrs. Vanrensselaer Vanzandt Van Twiller. I cannot say. But one evening the whole club knew the entire story.

Van Twiller had actually been very deeply interested—but not in any real actress. No, he'd been interested in Mademoiselle Olympe Zabriski. Drama was not her walk in life. It was her feats on the trapeze that attracted Van Twiller. (Although these same feats had failed to interest Delaney and me that night we wandered into the uptown theater).

That a man like Van Twiller should be fascinated by a common circus-girl seems simply unbelievable. But how often the unbelievable happens! Besides, Mademoiselle Olympe was not a common circus-girl. She was a most daring athlete of great beauty and grace. She was a figure out of Greek mythology. High up there above the gaslights, she glowed in the air like a golden arrow.

I am describing Mademoiselle Olympe as she appeared to Van Twiller when he first walked into the theater. To me she seemed to be a girl of 18 or 20. Of course she could have been much older. Make-up and distance keep these people forever young. She was small, finely built, and rather pretty. But she plainly showed the effects of hard physical work. Van Twiller admired her hard work. "If I had a daughter, I wouldn't send her to a boarding school," he used to say. "I'd send her to a gym. Our American women have no muscle. They are lilies, pale, pretty—and so weak. You marry an American woman, and what do you marry? A headache. Look at English girls. They are roses, and they last the season through."

Walking home from the theater that first night, Van Twiller's mind was filled with the girl. If only he could give her set of nerves and muscles to any one of 200 high-bred women he knew! Why, he would marry that woman on the spot.

The following evening he went to see Mademoiselle Olympe again. "Olympe Zabriski," he whispered as he entered the lobby. "What a strange name! Olympe is French. Zabriski is Polish. It is her stage name, of course. Her real name is probably Sarah Jones. What kind of creature can she be in private life? I wonder if she wears that costume all the time. Does she spring to her meals from a high bar?" Van Twiller went on this way until the curtain rose.

This was on a Friday. There was a show the next afternoon, and he went to that, too. He also had a seat for the next evening's entertainment. He began dropping into the theater for half an hour every night just to watch her act. He was surprised when he realized that he had not missed Mademoiselle Olympe's show for nearly two weeks.

"This will never do," said Van Twiller. "Olympe"—he called her Olympe as if she were an old friend—"is a wonderful creature. But this will never do. Van, my boy, you must stop this altogether."

But half past nine that night found him in his box seat. And so it went for another week. In the beginning a habit leads a man gently with silken threads. But by and by those soft silk threads become iron chains!

A new feeling came over Van Twiller as he watched Mademoiselle Olympe's feats. Now he began to fear that she might slip from that swinging bar. One of the thin cords might snap, letting her drop, head first, from the dizzy height. He would imagine her lying in a glittering heap at the footlights.

Oh, hers was a hard, bitter life! Nothing but poverty and a miserable home could have driven her to it. What if she should end it all some night by just unclasping that little hand? It looked so small and white from the box where Van Twiller was sitting!

That frightful idea fascinated while it chilled him. Now it was nearly impossible for him to stay away from the theater. In the beginning, his pastime had not kept him from his usual social pleasures. But soon he only wanted to walk the streets alone until it was time for her show. So he stayed away from his friends. He was missed, and everyone at the club began to talk about him.

I find it hard to explain now what Van Twiller was unable to explain himself. He was not in love with Mademoiselle Olympe. He had no wish to speak to her or to hear her speak. A Van Twiller friendly with a female acrobat? Good heavens! Even he knew that that was impossible. Taken down from the trapeze-bar, Olympe Zabriski would have shocked every well-bred bone in Van Twiller's body. He was simply fascinated by her grace and wild spirit. And no society gossip could have been harder on Van Twiller than he was on himself. To be so attracted, and to know it, is something of a punishment for a proud man. So Van Twiller took his punishment and went to the theater every evening.

"When her show's run is over, this business will be finished," he thought.

Mademoiselle Olympe's show finally did close. She left town. But the act had drawn crowds to the uptown theater. Before Van Twiller could get over missing her, she had returned. Her reopening was advertised on posters.

On a brick wall opposite the windows of Van Twiller's bedroom a huge circus poster was put up. On it was printed MADEMOISELLE OLYMPE ZABRISKI in letters at least a foot high. This thing stared him in the face when he woke up one morning. He felt as if she had called on him overnight and left her card. He promised himself he would not repeat the mistake of the last month.

The evening came when Mademoiselle Olympe was to again appear. Van Twiller dined at the club. Feeling more like himself than he had felt in weeks, he returned to his rooms. He put on his slippers, took up a good book, and began reading.

Then the lively French clock on the mantel struck nine. Van Twiller looked up. The clock was set in a bronze carving of Mercury. The god's arms spread gracefully in the air. It looked somewhat like Mademoiselle Olympe flying on her trapeze! When the clock struck the next half-hour, Van Twiller rose from his chair like a machine. He slid his feet into his walking shoes. He threw his overcoat across his arm. And he walked out of the room. Soon Van Twiller found himself taking his seat in a private box. And night after night he returned during the second round of the performances of Mademoiselle Olympe.

Van Twiller was even worse this second time. He not only went to every show. He also thought of Olympe a number of times between breakfast and dinner. And he began to spend hours at night dreaming of her. It was always the same frightening dream. Van Twiller would imagine himself seated at the theater watching Mademoiselle Olympe as usual. All the members of Our Club were there. Suddenly the young lady would leap from her trapeze. She would come flying through the air, hurtling toward his private box. Then the unhappy man would wake up with cold drops standing out on his forehead.

Now as for Mademoiselle Olympe, she knew nothing of Van Twiller. She just went along drawing her pay. She was completely unaware that a miserable slave was wearing her chains in the theater every night.

Now Van Twiller never made himself known to the lady. That shows that he was not in love. But what if Van Twiller had not been Van Twiller—but a poor man of no family and no position? And what if New York had been Paris? But it is useless to guess what might have happened. What *did* happen is enough.

It happened during the second week

of Mademoiselle Olympe's second appearances. A whisper made its way up the Hudson to a grand mansion standing on the river bank. The whisper told the lady living there that all was not well with the last of the Van Twillers. He was becoming a stranger to his old friends. He was wasting every evening in a playhouse. And not only that, he was watching an unladylike young woman hang from a piece of wood attached to two ropes!

Mrs. Van Twiller came down to town by the next train. She came to look into this matter.

When she arrived, the flower of the family was having breakfast in his cozy apartment on 34th Street. She came right out with the rumor that had been reported to her. When he told her the whole story of Mademoiselle Zabriski, she was pleased, but not too much pleased. Two or three times during his story, the mother had some trouble holding back a laugh. She thought about it for a few minutes. Then she invited

Van Twiller to return with her the next day up the Hudson and visit his home. He accepted the invitation, for he could not refuse.

When this was settled, the lady left and Van Twiller went straight to the shop of Ball, Black, and Company. There he chose the finest diamond bracelet he could find. For his mother? Dear me, no! She already had the family jewelry.

I would not like to state the huge sum Van Twiller paid for this bracelet. It had diamonds that would have quickened the pulse of any wrist. It was such a bracelet as a prince might have sent to a princess.

In the bracelet's soft leather case, Van Twiller placed his card. On the back of it he had written a few lines. It begged Mademoiselle Olympe Zabriski to accept a small gift from one who had watched her with interest and pleasure. "Of course I must enclose my card, as I would to any lady," Van Twiller had said to himself.

The package sent off, Van Twiller felt easier in his mind. He owed the girl for many pleasant hours that might otherwise have passed heavily. He had paid the debt. He had paid it like a prince, as a Van Twiller should. He spent the rest of the day at the club and in making a few purchases for his trip. The thought that his trip up the Hudson was a clumsy escape only came to him unpleasantly from time to time.

When he returned to his room late at night, he found a note lying on the writing table. He jumped as his eye caught the words *Majestic Theater*. They were stamped in red letters on the corner of the envelope. Van Twiller broke the seal with shaking fingers.

Now, some time afterwards, this note fell into the hands of Livingstone. He showed it to Stuyvesant, who showed it to Delaney, who showed it to me. I copied it down. The note ran as follows:

Mr. Van Twiller Dear Sir - i am verry greatfull to you for that Bracelett. it come just in the nic of time for me. The

Mademoiselle Zabriski thing is about played out. my beard is getting too much for me. i shall have to grow a mustash and take to some other line of busyness. i dont no what now, but will let you no. You wont feel bad if i sell that Bracelett, will you? I can git a fair sum for it. Pleas accept my thanks for your Beautiful and Unexpected present.

 Youre respectfull servent,
 Charles Montmorenci Walters

The next day Van Twiller was more than willing to spend a few weeks with his mother at the family home.

And then he went to Europe.

Thinking About
the Stories

Marjorie Daw

1. Some stories are not told in a conventional sense. How is this story told? How does reading letters between John Flemming and Edward Delaney make you, the reader, feel? Does Jack seem like someone you know, or is he just a character?

2. Interesting story plots often have unexpected twists and turns. What surprises did you find in this story? Was the outcome what you expected?

A Struggle for Life

1. Who is telling this story? Is the narrator the same person as the storyteller? Why does Mr. Hall tell his neighbor such a fascinating tale?

2. Philip Wentworth was devastated to learn that his love, Julie Dorine, was dead. How did his attitude toward life change when he was locked in the tomb? Why did it change? Explain your answer.

Mademoiselle Olympe Zabriski

1. Are there friends or enemies in this story? Who are they? What forces do you think keep the friends together and the enemies apart?

2. Suppose this story had a completely different outcome. Can you think of another effective ending for this story?